TYRANNOSAURUS

ANCHISAURUS

STEGOSAURUS

BRONTOSAURUS

TRICERATOPS

SCELIDOSAURUS

TYRANNOSAURUS

BRONTOSAURUS

ANCHISAURUS

SCELIDOSAURUS

TRICERATOPS

TYRANNOSAURUS

STEGOSAURUS

ANCHISAURUS

For Tom,
who introduced his bucketful of dinosaurs
to Ann and me one lucky Sunday afternoon
at The Chelsea Gardener
—*I.W.*

For William
—*A.R.*

Text copyright © 1999 by Ian Whybrow
Illustrations copyright © 1999 by Adrian Reynolds
First American edition 1999 published by Orchard Books
First published in Great Britain in 1999 by David & Charles Children's Books

Ian Whybrow and Adrian Reynolds assert the right to be identified as the author
and the illustrator of this work.

Orchard Books, A Grolier Company
95 Madison Avenue, New York, NY 10016

Manufactured in Italy
The text of this book is set in 21 point Goudy.
The illustrations are watercolor.
1 3 5 7 9 10 8 6 4 2

Library of Congress Cataloging-in-Publication Data
Whybrow, Ian.
Sammy and the dinosaurs / by Ian Whybrow ; illustrated by Adrian Reynolds.—
1st American edition.
p.   cm.
Summary: Sammy finds toy dinosaurs in the attic that come to life when he names each one.
ISBN 0-531-30207-5
[1. Dinosaurs—Fiction. 2. Toys—Fiction.] I. Reynolds, Adrian, ill. II. Title.
PZ7.W6225Sam 1999 [E]—dc21 99-22387

Sammy
and the
Dinosaurs

by Ian Whybrow

illustrated by Adrian Reynolds

Orchard Books
New York

Gran thought the attic needed a cleaning.
She let Sammy help.
Sammy found an old box
all covered with dust.

He lifted the lid . . .
DINOSAURS!

Sammy took the
dinosaurs downstairs.

He unbent the
bent ones.

He fixed the
broken ones.

He got up on a chair and washed them in the sink.
Gran came to see. "Just what do you think you're up to?"
she said.

"Dinosaurs don't like boxes," Sammy said.
"They want to be in a bucket."

Meg came in from watching TV.
She said it was stupid, fussing over so much junk.
"Dinosaurs *aren't* junk," Sammy said.

The next day, he went to the library with Mom.
He took the dinosaurs in their bucket.

Sammy found out all the names in a book
and told them to the dinosaurs.
He whispered to each one:

"You are my Scelidosaurus.
  You are my Stegosaurus.
    You are my Triceratops."

And there were enough names for all of the dinosaurs:
the Brontosaurus, the Anchisaurus, and the Tyrannosaurus.
The dinosaurs said: "Thank you, Sammy."
They said it very quietly, but just
loud enough for Sammy to hear.

They went to the beach.

When Sammy had a bath, the dinosaurs had a bath.

When Sammy went to bed, the dinosaurs went to bed.

Sometimes they got left behind.
But they were never lost for long,
because Sammy knew all their names.

And he always called out their names
just to make sure they were safe.

One day, Sammy went on a
train with Gran.
He was so excited, he forgot all
about the bucket.

Gran dried his eyes.
"Never mind," she said.
"I'll buy you a nice new video."

Sammy watched the video with Meg.
It was nice, but not like the dinosaurs.

At bedtime, Sammy said to Mom, "I like videos.
But I like my dinosaurs better,
    because you can fix them,
        you can bathe them,
            you can take them to bed.

And best of all, you can say their names."

Sammy was still upset the next morning.
Meg said, "Dusty old junk!"
That was why Meg's book got milk on it.
Gran took Sammy to his room to settle down.

Later Gran took Sammy to the train station
to see the Lost and Found man.
The man said, "Dinosaurs? Yes, we have found some dinosaurs.
But how do we know they are *your* dinosaurs?"

Sammy said, "I will close my eyes
and call their names.
Then you will know."

And he closed his eyes and called their names.
He called:

"Come back

my Scelidosaurus!"

"Come back my Stegosaurus!"

"Come back my Triceratops!"

He called "come back" to all the dinosaurs:
    the Brontosaurus
        and the Anchisaurus
            and the Tyrannosaurus
                and all the rest of the lost, old dinosaurs.

And when he opened his eyes . . .

. . . there they were—all of them, standing on the counter next to the bucket.

"All correct!" said the man.
"These are definitely your dinosaurs! Definitely!"

And the dinosaurs whispered to Sammy.
They whispered very quietly,
but just loud enough for Sammy to hear:

"You are definitely our Sammy. Definitely."

Going home from the station,
Sammy was very happy.
Gran said to the neighbor, "Our Sammy
likes those old dinosaurs!"

"Definitely," whispered Sammy.
"And my dinosaurs definitely like me."

ENDOSAURUS.

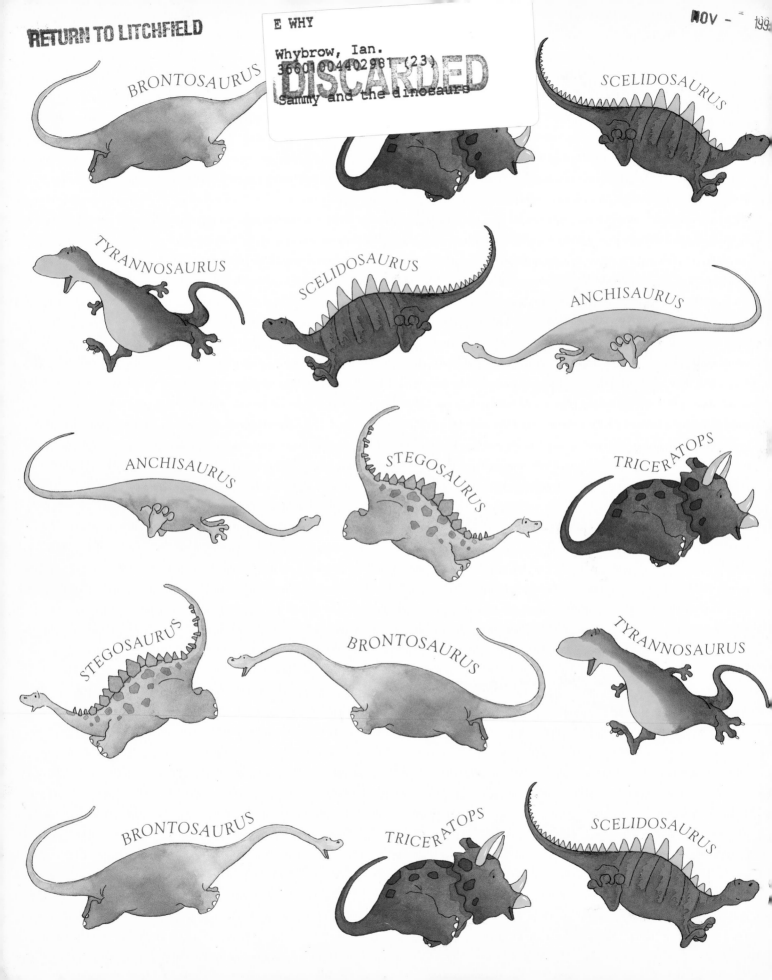

BRONTOSAURUS

SCELIDOSAURUS

TYRANNOSAURUS

SCELIDOSAURUS

ANCHISAURUS

ANCHISAURUS

STEGOSAURUS

TRICERATOPS

STEGOSAURUS

BRONTOSAURUS

TYRANNOSAURUS

BRONTOSAURUS

TRICERATOPS

SCELIDOSAURUS